Special thanks to Liss Norton

To B.S. with lots of love

ORCHARD BOOKS

First published in Great Britain in 2013 by Orchard Books
This edition published in 2017 by The Watts Publishing Group

7 9 10 8 6

© 2013 Hothouse Fiction Limited
Illustrations © Orchard Books 2013

A CIP catalogue record for this book is available from the British Library.

ISBN 978 1 40832 336 6

Printed in Great Britain by Clays Ltd, St Ives plc

The paper and board used in this book are made from wood from responsible sources

Orchard Books
An imprint of Hachette Children's Group
Part of The Watts Publishing Group Limited
Carmelite House, 50 Victoria Embankment, London EC4Y 0DZ

An Hachette UK Company
www.hachette.co.uk
www.hachettechildrens.co.uk

Series created by Hothouse Fiction
www.hothousefiction.com

Christmas Ballerina

ROSIE BANKS

ORCHARD

This is the Secret Kingdom

Christmas Castle

Book
One

Contents

⌒Christmas Decorations⌒

"Oh, *no!*" giggled Jasmine Smith. "It's gone wrong again!" She tossed some scraps of white paper up in the air and watched as they fluttered down.

Her friends Ellie Macdonald and Summer Hammond laughed as well. It was Christmas Eve and they were all sitting on the floor in Ellie's lounge,

making some last-minute decorations
with Ellie's little sister, Molly. Jasmine was
trying to make snowflakes by snipping
folded paper into lacy shapes, but all
she'd ended up with so far was a big,
messy mound of cuttings.

"Yours look so beautiful, Ellie," Jasmine
sighed. She picked up one of Ellie's
lacy snowflakes
and held it
against the
window so the
winter sunshine
streamed through
the holes. "When
these are covered
in glitter, they'll
look just like real
snowflakes."

"Why don't you help me and Molly make paper chains, Jasmine?" suggested Summer. "They're much easier than snowflakes." She held up one of the colourful paper chains they'd made.

"Do you remember that snowflake dance we did at school a couple of Christmases ago?" Ellie asked. "You were the chief snowflake, weren't you, Jasmine?"

Molly laughed as Jasmine jumped up and twirled across the room, her long dark hair streaming out behind her. "We danced like this," Jasmine said, remembering. "And then…" She sprang forward with her arms arched above her head and knocked into the Christmas tree. "Whoa!" she gasped as it began to wobble.

Ellie and Summer jumped up and caught the tree just in time.

"That was lucky!" giggled Summer. "Your mum wouldn't have been very pleased if it had fallen over, Ellie. It might have squashed all your presents!"

"Sorry," Jasmine said, grinning apologetically. "I suppose there's not really enough space in here for dancing."

As Summer straightened the tree, one very special decoration caught her eye. Molly must have noticed it too because she came up and gently touched it, her green eyes sparkling.

"It's so pretty," She smiled. "Is it a fairy?"

"She's a pixie," Summer explained, showing her the sparkling glass ornament. "See, she's riding on a leaf."

"Look, Mum!" Molly cried as her mum came in with some mince pies. "A pixie!" She pointed at the decoration.

"Oh, that's lovely." Ellie's mum smiled. "Almost as nice as your paper chains and snowflakes! I don't remember seeing that one before. I wonder where we got it?"

The girls exchanged a glance and Ellie smothered a giggle. She knew exactly where it had come from – the Secret Kingdom! Santa Claus himself had given it to her after she, Summer and Jasmine had saved Christmas there last year.

"Molly, do you want to help me in the kitchen?" Ellie's mum asked. "We might be able to find some hot chocolate to go with the mince pies."

"Okay!" Molly grinned.

As soon as Molly and her mum

had left, Ellie turned to her friends. "I wonder what's happening in the Secret Kingdom?" she thought out loud.

The girls were the only people who knew about King Merry's special world, where pixies, brownies, elves, unicorns and all kinds of other amazing creatures lived. The Secret Kingdom was the most wonderful place ever, and at Christmas time it was even more magical!

"Trixi must be getting ready for Christmas, too," said Summer. Their pixie friend, Trixibelle, was King Merry's assistant. Whenever there were problems in the Secret Kingdom, she sent them a message through the Magic Box, the only one of King Merry's inventions that actually worked! King Merry had made it when his mean sister Queen Malice had tried to take over the kingdom and make everyone miserable, and it had found the only three people who could help – Jasmine, Summer and Ellie!

Ellie smiled. "Last Christmas was amazing, wasn't it?"

"You can say that again!" agreed Jasmine. "I bet everyone's at Christmas Castle already, sitting round the fire singing *Jingle Elves!*"

"Or *Hark the Herald Mermaids Sing!*"
Summer added.

The girls all grinned as they remembered the golden castle where King Merry always spent Christmas. It was covered in holly and ivy, and the most beautiful decorations, and there were always lots of elves, mermaids, nymphs, unicorns and pixies, playing games and singing carols. Best of all, Santa was there! He was King Merry's second cousin, twice removed, and he always spent Christmas Day in the Secret Kingdom.

Summer tucked a strand of long blonde hair behind her ear and sighed. "I wish we could go back and see them this year."

Ellie dived under the Christmas tree and rustled around in the presents. She brought out a beautiful wooden box carved with unicorns, mermaids and pixies. On the curved lid was a beautiful mirror surrounded by six green gems that twinkled when they caught the light.

"The Magic Box!" Summer breathed excitedly.

"I wish Trixi would send us a message," Ellie said longingly. "I keep checking the mirror and thinking it's glowing, then realising it's just the reflection of the Christmas lights."

"Look!" cried Jasmine eagerly. "It's

glowing now!"

"No, it's the tree lights," Ellie said, pointing at the colourful lights that twinkled and flickered around the tree. "See?" She tilted the box away from the tree, but light went on shining from the mirror. "Oh!" she gasped, a tingle of excitement running through her. "It really *is* a message!"

The girls exchanged delighted looks. "Brilliant!" Jasmine grinned as they gathered round the box. "It looks as though we'll be going to the Secret Kingdom this Christmas after all!"

A Christmas Riddle

Ellie read out the riddle, her voice shaking with excitement:

"Dear friends, please come and join us here
In a golden castle full of cheer
For a Festive Feast and lots of fun,
With happy times for everyone!"

"That *has* to be Christmas Castle!" Summer grinned.

"Of course!" Jasmine and Ellie cheered together, overjoyed at the idea of going back there.

The girls quickly placed their hands over the green gems surrounding the mirror. "The answer is Christmas Castle!" they cried together.

The box flew open, pouring golden light into the room. Glittering silver snowflakes fluttered in the stream of light, then began to whirl around the room, throwing sparkling lacy patterns across the walls.

For a moment, nothing seemed to happen. Then the pixie ornament on the Christmas tree started to glow. Jasmine blinked as it got brighter and brighter, then rubbed her eyes in amazement. Instead of just one pixie, suddenly there

were two pixies there! Next to the
ornament was a *real* pixie, flying on a
glossy holly leaf with a cluster of plump
red berries attached to the stalk.
She had twinkling blue eyes and
pointy ears that peeked out from
under a tangle of
blonde hair.
She was wearing
a red dress
made of
velvety rose
petals and
spangled
with tiny
gold stars, and
matching red
shoes with gold
laces. On her head

was a pair of joke reindeer antlers.

"Trixibelle!" Summer cheered.

"Merry Christmas, Trixi!" Ellie laughed, "I like your antlers!"

Trixi beamed round. "Merry Christmas!" she cried. She steered her leaf to each of them in turn and kissed them on the tips of their noses.

"What's happening in the Secret Kingdom?" Jasmine asked. "Queen Malice hasn't done anything horrid has she?"

Ellie and Summer looked at each other anxiously. The nasty queen disliked fun and laughter, so she *hated* Christmas.

"I'm not sure." Trixi looked worried. "The Festive Feast should be starting soon at Christmas Castle, but King

Merry's special guest, Rosalind Daintyfeet, hasn't arrived. She's the most famous elf ballerina in the whole of the Secret Kingdom and everyone's been looking forward to her Christmas Day performance. But she was meant to get to the castle yesterday, and no one's heard from her. She's disappeared!"

"Don't worry Trixi," Summer comforted her. "I'm sure she'll turn up soon."

"I hope so," Trixi replied, twirling her leaf in a pirouette. "I've been so excited about meeting her!"

"A Christmas adventure *and* a ballerina!" Jasmine grinned. "It's like all my Christmas wishes have come true!"

"We'd better go quickly," Ellie said, glancing at the door. She knew no time would pass here while they were in the

Secret Kingdom, but she didn't want her sister to burst in and see a real pixie!

The girls joined hands and waited excitedly while Trixi tapped her beautiful glittery pixie ring. She chanted:

"Christmas Castle's the place to be.
Magic us there speedily!"

As she spoke, her words appeared in the box's mirror then swirled up into the air, breaking into hundreds of shimmering sparkles. Twinkling snowflakes came whooshing out of the Magic Box. They fluttered around the room, twirling faster and faster until the girls were at the centre of a snowy whirlwind. They squeezed each other's hands tightly as it lifted them off their feet.

"Yippee!" cried Ellie. "We're off to the Secret Kingdom!"

As the whirling snowflakes cleared, the girls landed safely on a snowy path. Summer grinned in delight as she saw Christmas Castle up ahead. It looked just as beautiful as last year, surrounded by holly bushes smothered with bright red berries, and a huge green wreath dotted with red bows hung on the enormous front door. Thousands of tiny

fairy lights covered the golden walls,
and ivy garlands were draped across the
windowsills.

"I can't believe we're here again!"
Jasmine hugged her friends. "It's the most
Christmassy place ever!"

"And look at all this snow," said Ellie
excitedly, picking some up and throwing

a snowball at her friends.

Jasmine and Summer shrieked happily as they dodged the snow.

"I always wanted to have a white Christmas!" Summer squealed, gazing round eagerly. "Everything's so beautiful."

"But cold," giggled Ellie, puffing a cloud of breath into the chilly air. "Let's get inside."

As they hurried towards the castle, Jasmine felt something settle on her head. "My tiara!" She grinned. The girls' pretty jewelled tiaras appeared by magic whenever they arrived in the Secret Kingdom. They showed that they were Very Important Friends of King Merry. "Now I know an adventure's about to begin!"

The Snow Globe

As the castle doors opened, the girls
caught a glimpse of a long hallway full
of beautiful decorations. Then an excited
crowd of brownies, pixies and fairies,
all dressed in their best clothes, rushed
forward. There were nymphs in beautiful
dresses made out of leaves and ferns,
unicorns with Christmassy berries woven
into their manes, and snow brownies
wearing red velvet suits. All the children
were clutching toy ballerinas.

"Rosalind?" someone cried excitedly.

"Sorry, no," Jasmine replied.

"Hasn't she arrived yet?" Trixi asked with a frown.

The nearest brownie shook his head sadly.

"Ellie, Jasmine and Summer!" came a familiar voice. "Happy Christmas! Thank goodness you're here!" The crowd parted and King Merry came hurrying towards the girls. He was dressed in his purple robes, which were trimmed with soft white feathers, but underneath them he was wearing a cuddly jumper with a picture of a penguin on it.

"There you are, my dears," said King Merry, smiling at the girls. "I was so relieved when Trixi said she'd fetch you." He straightened his crown, which was perched on top of a Santa hat. "Has she told you about Rosalind?"

The girls nodded.

"She's the most beautiful ballerina in the whole land," King Merry told them, his rosy cheeks getting even pinker. "I can't think where she's got to," he added anxiously.

"Remember last year, when Queen Malice tried to ruin Christmas for everyone?" Ellie whispered to her friends. "Do you think she could have something to do with Rosalind's disappearance?"

"Let's hope not," said Summer with a shiver. "Queen Malice is the last person

I want to see on Christmas Eve!"

"We've got everything ready for Rosalind's arrival," King Merry told them. "Come and see!" The little king hurried them through the crowd and into the castle's enormous banqueting hall. Long tables ran the length of the room. They were covered in crisp white tablecloths and were laid with gold plates

and cutlery, red crackers, sparkling glasses and green napkins folded into the shape of mini Christmas trees. Red candles were set in tall, glittering holders that were twined with stems of holly and ivy, gold flowers and clusters of red berries. Above the tables hung crystal chandeliers that glittered in the sunshine pouring in at the windows.

"Doesn't it look lovely?" exclaimed Ellie.

"Later the tables will be magically filled with food," Trixi explained. "But nothing will appear until every single guest is sat down. The Festive Feast can't happen without Rosalind."

Next to the tables there was a huge Christmas tree that was actually growing out of the ground through a hole in the hall floor. It was so tall that it almost reached the ceiling, and it was beautifully decorated with hundreds of fairy lights and glittering baubles. Right at the top was the Shining Star, which Trixi lit every year to start the Christmas fun. It was gleaming brightly now, covering the room in Christmassy light.

As King Merry led them further into the hall, they saw that a huge snow globe had been set up on a stage at one end of the room.

"Amazing!" Jasmine gasped as King Merry led them into the globe through a little glass door in the back. Inside there was a gingerbread house with a snowy roof and window frames made of candy canes. The front door looked as though it was made of chocolate and the chimney was an enormous marshmallow topped with pink candyfloss smoke.

Another Christmas tree stood beside the house, its branches draped with strings of glistening pearls and twinkling fairy lights. Best of all, sparkly snow was falling gently inside the globe.

"Rosalind was supposed to be dancing inside this snow globe tomorrow," said Trixi sadly.

"Don't worry, Trixi," Summer said kindly. "She still will. Maybe we should go and look for her?"

"Yes, let's start looking now!" said Jasmine.

"She might just have got lost on the way here," suggested Ellie.

"What an excellent idea!" King Merry grinned. "She lives near Lily Pad Lake."

"Right, we'll head in that direction," said Jasmine. She smiled at King Merry. "We'll find her, even if we have to search the whole kingdom."

"Oh, thank you, my dears," said King Merry gratefully. "I knew we could count on you."

"If we're going out in the cold you'll need warmer clothes," Trixi said. She tapped her pixie ring, and in a flash the girls were dressed in warm cloaks with cosy fur-lined hoods. Jasmine smiled as she saw they each had a Christmas jumper like King Merry's. Hers had a snowflake pattern, Summer's had a cute

snow bear on it, and Ellie's had a huge
stripy candy cane.

They hurried back towards the castle
doors. But just as they reached them,
the doors were suddenly flung open. A
unicorn stood there panting, covered
in snow.

"A message! A message from Rosalind Daintyfoot!" he gasped. He looked around the room, then bowed to the king. "King Merry, my name is Proudhoof. I was one of the unicorns pulling Rosalind's carriage."

Summer rushed forward to put a blanket on Proudhoof's back, and an elf butler gave the exhausted unicorn some water.

Everyone waited anxiously while he drank. "Where is Rosalind?" King Merry asked.

"Is she okay?" Jasmine added.

The unicorn shook his head sadly. "The carriage was attacked by Storm Sprites," he said with an angry whinny. "I managed to get away, but—"

"They took Rosalind!" Ellie finished for him.

Proudhoof nodded. "They've taken her to Thunder Castle!"

Summer gasped. "But isn't that—"

"Where Queen Malice lives?" Jasmine finished.

The crowd all gave horrified gasps.

"Your Majesty." Proudhoof turned to King Merry and bowed low. "Queen Malice has kidnapped Rosalind!"

A Snowy Journey

Summer shuddered at the thought of
going to Queen Malice's home. If it was
anything like the wicked queen it was
sure to be a nasty place.

While brownies led the exhausted
unicorn away to rest, the girls and King
Merry thought about what to do.

"Can you magic us to Thunder Castle?" Jasmine asked Trixi.

Trixi shook her head. "Queen Malice protects her home with spells. I can't just magic us there," she replied. "But I do have an idea of how to get us there quickly." She tapped her pixie ring and chanted:

"Pixie magic, don't be slow.
We need some help to cross the snow!"

Silver sparkles flew out of the ring. They swirled round and round, then swooped towards the front door. Jasmine, Summer and Ellie ran after them and flung the door open. Outside, resting on the snow, were three beautifully carved wooden sledges.

"Brilliant!" cried Jasmine. "I love sledging!"

"This one's yours, Summer," Trixi said, pointing to a yellow sledge decorated with glittering blue stars.

"Thank you," Summer said, climbing on anxiously. She liked her sledge, but she felt terrified about where it was going to take her.

"I bet this one's mine," Jasmine said, running to stand beside a vivid pink sledge with a silver snowflake pattern.

"And this is mine," Ellie said, crouching down for a closer look at a purple sledge painted with green holly leaves.

"You're exactly right." Trixi smiled.

"Is it downhill all the way to Thunder

Castle?" Jasmine asked. "I mean, sledges only go downhill, don't they?"

"Not these ones," Trixi explained. "They're enchanted, so they'll go anywhere you want."

Summer looked at her friends anxiously. Now they were ready to go, even Jasmine looked a bit worried.

"Head for Thunder Castle!" Ellie called bravely. "We've got a ballerina to find!"

"Wait for me!" cried King Merry as the sledges glided forwards. "I'm coming with you. My horrid sister won't get away with this!"

The sledges skidded to a halt with a spray of snow, and Summer jumped off to help King Merry who was slipping and sliding as he walked along. "Would you like to ride with me?" she offered.

"Yes, please!" he said, patting Summer's
hand. "That would be lovely."

Summer sat down and King Merry
squeezed on behind her. "Away we go!"
he cried.

Soon they'd left Christmas Castle far
behind and were whizzing across fields,
with a blanket of white, glittering snow
stretching out in front of them.

In the far distance Magic Mountain rose up to meet the sky, which had faded from bright blue to pale grey, with streaks of darker purply-grey. The sun was sinking fast as night approached.

"Is that Rosalind?" Summer asked, spotting a ballerina toy that King Merry was holding. It was the same as the children had had at Christmas Castle.

"Yes." King Merry brought out the figurine. It was a dancing ballerina standing on tiptoe on a round base. King Merry tapped the base and the ballerina magically started to spin round and round so fast that she lifted up into the air.

"That's Rosalind's signature move – her air pirouette," King Merry explained sadly. "I was so looking forward to seeing it. Oh, I do hope that she's okay!"

"Look! Rosalind must have come this way!" Jasmine cried, pointing to some hoof prints in the snow. "Those are unicorn hoofprints. And there are the

tracks made by her carriage wheels."

"And look here," gasped Ellie. "Are those…"

"Storm Sprite footprints!" Summer gasped, looking at the pointy-toed footprints next to the wheel tracks. The footprints surrounded the wheels and then stopped.

"They must have climbed aboard the carriage," Jasmine said, peering at the footprints and feeling like a detective. "This way!" She pointed to where the tracks led off into the distance.

The sledges sped away, with Trixi zooming alongside. But now it began to snow, with big flakes whirling round them and making it hard to see where they were going. As the sun set the sky grew black, and the heavy clouds blotted out

the moon and stars. Soon they could see nothing but snowflakes.

"Hang on, there are some more tracks," Summer cried, pointing at two parallel lines in the snow. Next to them were another set of lines, and another. But there weren't any unicorn hoofprints.

"Oh, no!" Jasmine groaned. "Those are *our* tracks, from our sledges. We're going round in circles!"

"But how?" Ellie exclaimed.

"It must be part of Queen Malice's magic, protecting Thunder Castle," Trixi explained.

"This is hopeless!" sighed Ellie.

"We'll never find our way to Thunder Castle in the dark," said King Merry in a gloomy voice. "We'll have to turn back."

"But we can't leave Rosalind with

Queen Malice on Christmas Eve!"
Summer said desperately.

"Wait!" Ellie cried. "What's that noise?"

"Stop, sledges," commanded Jasmine.

The sledges slowed, then stopped
altogether. They listened hard, holding
their breath, and now they could all hear
it – silvery bells jingling in the darkness.

"It's coming from up in the sky," said
Ellie, puzzled.

They looked up, and Summer spotted
a faint pinprick of red light moving high
overhead. "There!" she said, pointing.
"But what on earth is it?"

They all stood up, craning their necks
to get a better view.

"It must be Rudolph's nose!" Jasmine
cried. "It's Santa!"

"Quick, we've got to get him to help
us," Summer gasped.

"Santa! Help!" they all yelled together.

The red light moved on.

"Santa!" the girls
shouted again,
louder than ever.

This time the
light began to
turn. It swept
round in a

semi-circle, then headed back towards them.

"Down here, Santa!" shouted Jasmine.

The red light seemed to grow bigger and the jingle of bells became louder as Santa's sleigh flew down. Soon they could

hear the creak of the reindeers' harnesses, then the light from Rudolph's nose lit up the magical flying sleigh. Santa leaned over the side and waved. "Ho, ho, ho, hello there," he called.

The girls waved back eagerly as the reindeer and the sleigh came whooshing down and landed lightly beside them.

The sleigh was painted red with glittery gold swirls along the sides. Santa, who was dressed in his familiar red suit and hat with white fur edging, was sitting in the driver's seat with bulging sacks of presents piled up behind him. "Bless me!" he exclaimed, his eyes lighting up beneath his bushy white eyebrows.

"It's Summer, Ellie and Jasmine! And Trixi and Cousin Merry, too." Beaming, he climbed down from his sleigh and smoothed down his white beard. The girls giggled as he stood next to King Merry. Santa and King Merry looked really similar with their white beards, tubby tummies, glasses and kind smiles.

"Hello, Santa," the girls chorused, running forward to hug him. The reindeer looked round at them, setting their harness bells jingling.

"Merry Christmas!" Santa bellowed happily. "I'm just setting off to deliver the presents!" He looked around at the girls and his cheery smile disappeared. "But whatever's the matter?"

"Oh, Santa," Summer cried. "We need your help!"

Santa's Sleigh and Rosalind's Carriage

"We're looking for Rosalind Daintyfeet, the ballerina," Summer explained to Santa. "Queen Malice has kidnapped her!"

"And taken her to Thunder Castle," Jasmine finished.

"Queen Malice's magic is keeping us away," Ellie added. "And it's too dark and snowy to see where we're going."

"Ho, ho, ho, that *is* a problem," Santa said thoughtfully, stroking his beard. "I must be able to help somehow. Hop aboard."

Jasmine and Summer gazed up at him, their hearts thumping with excitement.

"Are we going to ride in your sleigh?" gasped Jasmine.

"Of course," Santa said. "This may be the busiest night of the year for me, but I'm not going to let Queen Malice ruin Christmas for Rosalind, or anyone else!"

"But Malice's magic—" Trixi started.

"Ho, ho, ho!" Santa laughed. "My sleigh

can take me to any house, anywhere! I'll take you straight to Thunder Castle."

"Oh, thank you!" Jasmine cried, scrambling aboard the sleigh.

Summer followed and squeezed into the seat beside Santa.

Ellie gulped, then followed her. She didn't like heights, and the thought of whizzing up into the sky was scary. Summer noticed Ellie's nervousness and took her hand. "We've flown in Santa's sleigh before, remember," she whispered.

"Yes, but that was only from the roof of Christmas Castle to the ground." Ellie said in a wobbly voice. "This is *really* flying!"

"You'll be completely safe," Jasmine promised. "After all, you're flying with Santa Claus!"

Ellie couldn't help smiling. Of course nothing could go wrong with Santa there!

Trixi flew her leaf down next to them, and snuggled up on Summer's lap.

"Come on, Merry," said Santa. "There's plenty of room in the back for you."

King Merry climbed into the sleigh and sat down next to a large parcel wrapped in colourful paper. "But what about the sledges?" he asked.

"I'll send them back to Christmas Castle, Your Majesty," said Trixi. She tapped her magic ring and cried:

"Head for Christmas Castle! Go!
Sledges zoom across the snow."

Blue sparkles came whooshing out of

the ring and the sledges sped away, back
to Christmas Castle.

"We should go, too," said Jasmine.

"Hold tight, everyone," Santa said. He
shook the reins. "Now, Dasher! Now,
Dancer!" he cried as the sleigh raced
forward over the snow.

"Now, Prancer and Vixen!" cried
Summer delightedly.

"On, Comet! On, Cupid!" yelled
Jasmine.

"On, Donner and Blitzen!" called Ellie.

"And *goooo*, Rudolph!" they all
shouted together.

As the sleigh sped up, the girls saw
magic sparkles glittering around the
reindeers' hooves, then they were off the
ground and soaring into the sky through
a blizzard of whirling snowflakes, with

Rudolph's glowing nose lighting
their path.

Ellie closed her eyes for a moment,
afraid to think about how high they were
going. But Santa's sleigh felt solid and
safe, and she was holding hands tightly
with Jasmine and Summer. Cautiously
she opened her eyes, then found herself
smiling. She was really flying in Santa's

sleigh, and it was amazing!

Soon they were skimming just above the treetops, with Rudolph's nose shining through the driving snow, casting a pink glow on the ground below them.

"This is brilliant!" gasped Jasmine, pulling her cloak more tightly around her to keep out the cold.

"It is!" Summer agreed, her eyes shining with excitement. Even Ellie agreed.

Summer and Jasmine looked over the side of the sleigh, but there was no sign of Thunder Castle. King Merry leaned so far over that he almost fell out, but the girls caught him just in time. As they flew, the ground below changed to a dark rocky landscape, sprinkled with snow. Black rocks stuck out of the snow like sharks' fins.

Jasmine shuddered. "I've never seen a part of the Secret Kingdom that looks like this before," she said.

"We're getting closer to my sister's home," King Merry said grimly. "Nothing grows near Thunder Castle."

Suddenly Ellie spotted something in the distance. It was a massive shape even blacker than the night sky. As they got closer she could see twisted turrets, a black drawbridge and a dark moat. "Is that...?" she asked nervously.

"Thunder Castle," King Merry replied in a gloomy voice.

The castle loomed on top of a tall hill, its walls and windows black and forbidding. Down the hill there was a black path, and at the bottom of the path there were two huge, twisted gates like a

snarling mouth. They
were covered with
leering gargoyles
and lightning bolts.

The girls shivered.
"Doesn't it look
horrible?" Jasmine
whispered.

"It must be the only place in the whole
of the Secret Kingdom with no Christmas
decorations," Trixi said.

"It's probably even more horrible
inside," Ellie said miserably. The three
girls looked at the palace and shuddered.

"We *have* to find Rosalind!" Summer
declared.

"Wait!" Jasmine cried. "What's that
down there?"

They all peered down at the ground.

"There!" cried Summer, pointing. "It's Rosalind's unicorn carriage!"

The shimmering glass carriage, which was decorated with beautifully carved pink roses, was lying deserted at the bottom of the rocks that led up to the huge black gates. There was one unicorn in the harness, whinnying anxiously and pawing the ground. As they watched, there was a movement from inside the carriage.

"Rosalind!" Trixi gasped.

"Here we go!" Santa cried. He pulled
on the reins and the reindeer galloped
towards the ground. Santa's sleigh landed
next to the carriage, sending up a spray
of snow.

The unicorn looked up as they landed.
"Help him," Jasmine shouted to King
Merry and Trixi. "We'll get Rosalind."

"Rosalind!" Ellie called as they ran
up to the carriage. Summer and Jasmine
raced after her.

As they reached the carriage, the door
was flung open. A black boot stepped
out, followed by a huge black skirt, and a
cloud of frizzy black hair.

"Rosalind?" Summer stuttered as the
figure emerged.

"No!" Queen Malice cackled. "ME!"

The Unicorn Carriage

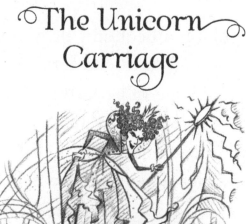

"You fools!" Queen Malice screeched. "You're too late! Soon Rosalind will be mine. As soon as she steps through the gates of Thunder Castle, she can never leave. She'll be trapped here forever!"

She pointed up at the huge gates. They were covered with gargoyles with their tongues stuck out. Struggling up towards them, the girls could see three Storm

Sprites pulling a beautiful elf. She wore a glittering pink tutu and a tiara, ballet slippers and cape of perfectly white fur.

"Help!" she shouted as the Storm Sprites dragged her along, their leathery bat-like wings flapping. "Please, help!"

"Rosalind!" Summer gasped.
"Get off her!" Jasmine shouted.
"Leave her alone!" Ellie yelled.

The girls started scrambling over the rocks after them.

"You'll never make it!" Queen Malice cackled as they ran. "She won't be dancing this Christmas – or *ever again!*"

Summer scowled at the wicked queen, and then gasped as Malice's words gave her an idea. *Rosalind's dance!* She raced after the others. "Rosalind, your pirouette!" she shouted as she ran. "Do your air pirouette!"

For a terrible second, she didn't think Rosalind had heard her. Summer, Jasmine and Ellie watched in horror as the sprites reached the gates. But just as they tried to pull Rosalind in, the elf ballerina started to spin. The snow whipped around her as she went up on the tips of her toes and twirled, faster and faster.

"What are you doing?" one of the sprites yelled.

"I can't hold on!" another shouted as Rosalind twisted even faster, until her feet left the ground.

"I'm so dizzy!" cried another.

The Storm Sprites let go and fell in a heap around the spinning ballerina. Delicately, Rosalind's feet touched back down on the black rock, and her spin slowed, a beautiful smile on her face.

"Run!" Jasmine yelled.

Rosalind glanced at the dizzy sprites, then started to race down the rocks towards the girls.

"Nooooo!" shrieked Queen Malice. She thumped her thunderbolt staff down so hard that the glass carriage shattered.

Jasmine, Summer and Ellie grinned as they reached the graceful ballerina. "Thank you so much!" Rosalind gasped as she met them.

"Don't thank us yet," Jasmine said as she took the beautiful ballerina's hand. "We've still got to get out of here."

"Ho, ho, ho, I can help with that!" came a jolly voice next to them as Santa sped up on his sleigh. Jasmine climbed aboard, then helped the others in. King Merry and Trixi were already there, and Rosalind's unicorn was in the back, lying happily next to all the Christmas presents.

"You idiots!" Queen Malice screeched at the dizzy sprites. "Rosalind Daintyfeet was all I wanted, and what do I get? Santa and my idiot brother! Not to mention those meddling girls from the

Other Realm and that pesky pixie! Do
I have to do everything myself?"

Raising her staff, she fired a thunderbolt
at Santa's sleigh.

"Duck!" cried Santa as the bolt
whizzed overhead.

"Let's go!" Ellie cried.

Santa flicked the reins and the reindeer began to run, their hooves glittering with magic. The sleigh skimmed across the snow beneath them. "Up!" Santa called.

The reindeer pawed the air and the sleigh took off, leaving a trail of magic sparkles behind it.

Queen Malice and her Storm Sprites watched angrily as the sleigh took off.

"Ho, ho, ho! Merry Christmas, Queen Malice!" Santa called. As the sleigh rose into the air, Santa waved his hand and suddenly strings of fairy lights, tinsel strands and brightly coloured streamers rained down over Thunder Castle. In a moment the castle's walls and turrets were covered with beautiful Christmas decorations. The pattern on the gates transformed from gargoyles and lightning bolts to smiling elves and candy canes, decorated with sparkling fairy lights.

"Aaaggghhhhh!" Queen Malice
screeched, shaking her fist at him. "Look
what you've done to my castle!" She
grabbed a string of fairy lights and
tried to yank them down, but they were
caught on the tip of the gates. "Get
them off!" she yelled at her
Storm Sprites with
an angry shriek.

The sprites
flapped up to the
gates and started
tearing down the
lights.

"Thanks, Santa," giggled Summer.

"I think Queen Malice was in need of
a bit of Christmas spirit," chuckled Santa.
"Now, I've got a busy night ahead of me
and you have a feast to go to! I'll drop

you off at Christmas Castle on the way."

The last thing Summer saw as they swooped away through the sky was Queen Malice furiously pulling the beautiful decorations from her castle gates.

Summer looked at her best friends and Rosalind, and they all giggled.

"Thank you so much for saving me," Rosalind said, smiling at them all in turn. "I never would have thought of using my pirouette if you hadn't been there."

"You're welcome." Jasmine grinned. "It's so lovely to meet you. We've heard lots about you."

"We couldn't just leave you with Queen Malice!" Summer added.

"And now we can have the Festive Feast," Ellie said happily.

The girls snuggled down in Santa's sleigh. They had Rosalind back and the Christmas fun could begin!

Soon they could see the beautiful lights of Christmas Castle below. Santa landed his sleigh in the garden, and they all hopped out. "Thank you, Santa," the girls chorused.

Santa beamed at them, his eyes twinkling kindly. "You're welcome. I'd better get going. I'm due in New Zealand very soon. The children there will be asleep already!"

"Will we see you tomorrow?" Summer asked hopefully.

"Oh, yes, Santa, you must come to my dance," Rosalind said, reaching up on tiptoe to kiss him on his rosy cheek.

Santa blushed bright red. "Of course I will. And I'll be seeing you all before then too," he said. "But you'll be fast asleep, of course!" He shook the reins. "Ho, ho, ho! Off we go," he cried.

The reindeer took off, and the sleigh circled above Christmas Castle as Santa waved cheerfully. "Merry Christmas!" he called as he zoomed away across the sky, leaving a wide path of magic stars behind him.

"We're back!" King Merry cried happily, opening the castle door. "And Rosalind is here at last. Let the Festive Feast begin!"

The Festive Feast

A huge cheer went up as Rosalind
pirouetted into Christmas Castle,
followed by the girls, King Merry and
Trixi. The crowd of brownies, pixies and
fairies who'd been waiting for Rosalind
to arrive beamed delightedly, and the
children all held up their ballerina dolls.

Rosalind smiled at them all, and rushed to thank Proudhoof, who whinnied happily when he saw her.

The girls quickly slipped off their boots, cloaks and gloves and handed them to the elf butlers.

"This way," cried King Merry, offering his arm to Rosalind.

"Thank you, Your Majesty." She smiled, curtseying low.

The girls followed her and King Merry to the banqueting hall, with the crowd skipping along behind them and chattering excitedly about the feast.

King Merry and Rosalind led everyone over to the table. Trixi showed the girls to their seats.

Everyone stood by their chair and King Merry tapped a spoon on his glass.

"Now that we are all here," he said, smiling at Rosalind and the girls, "the Festive Feast can begin! Please, take your places."

They sat down, and instantly the table sparkled with magic.

As soon as the sparkles cleared, the room filled with the delicious smell of Christmas goodies. Ellie, Summer and Jasmine gasped. The table was full of amazing food! There was every type of Christmas food that the girls had at home, as well as some they'd never seen before. There was a huge turkey surrounded by balls of stuffing and bacon curls, an enormous ham studded with cherries, bowls piled high with golden roast potatoes and a gigantic, round Christmas pudding.

Golden platters held dainty, star-shaped mince pies and stacks of chocolates wrapped in shiny red foil. Right in the middle of the table sat a beautifully iced Christmas cake, topped with a model of Christmas Castle and a teeny tiny figure of King Merry. It was even wearing his penguin jumper!

"Everything looks delicious," said Jasmine, licking her lips.

Everybody started pulling their crackers, filling the room with loud bangs and thousands of magical sparkles. Summer was sitting opposite Grandmother Aura, an imp they'd met on one of their adventures, and they pulled their crackers together. Jasmine pulled hers with Rosalind, and Ellie pulled hers with a brownie who burst out laughing whenever she told a joke.

"Look, my hat's a Christmas tree," giggled Summer, pulling the pointy green hat on over her tiara.

"Mine's a Christmas star," Ellie said, putting it on.

Jasmine's hat was shaped like a Christmas pudding. "It even *smells* Christmassy," she grinned.

Rosalind gave a tinkling laugh as she saw her hat was a spiky crown like Queen Malice's. The girls laughed as she screwed up her face and gave a cackle just like the horrid queen.

Soon the excited chatter died down as everyone tucked in.

"These frosted cherries are yummy," Jasmine said.

"So is this marshmallow cake," said Ellie, taking a huge bite.

"I'm looking forward to a piece of Christmas pudding," said Trixi. "And have you tasted the chocolate mince pies?"

"Yes, yummy!" said Jasmine.

"The ice cream fountain looks amazing," Summer said, watching the runny ice cream shoot high up in the air, then splash down into bowls, where it immediately froze.

"I'd like some of that too," said Jasmine, "but I'm already stuffed! I'm not sure I've got room for anything else."

"Just wait until tomorrow." King Merry chuckled. "The Christmas Day feast will be even better than this one."

"You will come tomorrow, won't you?" Rosalind asked, smiling. "I'd love you to see my show. After all, it's only going ahead thanks to you three girls." She shivered. "If you hadn't found me I'd be spending a very miserable Christmas in the dungeons at Thunder Castle."

"We'd love to come!" Jasmine exclaimed. She grinned at Ellie and Summer. "Wouldn't we?"

"You bet!" they agreed.

"I'll send you a message at three o'clock tomorrow," Trixi promised. "But

now I'd better get you home."

She kissed them on the tips of their noses. "Thanks for helping."

"We've really enjoyed it," said Ellie. "An adventure in the Secret Kingdom is a great way to start Christmas!"

The girls stood up and joined hands, then Trixi tapped her magic ring. A fountain of pink sparkles came whooshing up from the floor. They spun around the girls, lifting them off their feet.

"Bye, everyone," called Summer. "See you all tomorrow!"

When the sparkles vanished, they were back in Ellie's living room again. "Wow!" exclaimed Ellie. "That was so exciting! And we'll be going back to the Secret Kingdom again tomorrow."

"To see Rosalind dance," Jasmine said. "I can't wait!"

"Neither can I," said Summer. She scooped up her paper chains and picked up her coat.

"What are you doing?" Jasmine asked as she tucked into a mince pie. "It's not time to go yet."

"It is," giggled Summer. "I want to go to bed extra early tonight so tomorrow will come sooner!"

They all laughed. "Sleep tight then," said Ellie.

"I will," Summer said. "And I'll dream about another Secret Kingdom adventure!"

Book
Two

Contents

Christmas Day

"Oh, no!" groaned Ellie. She was playing snakes and ladders with her little sister Molly and had just landed on the longest snake on the board.

Molly giggled, setting her red curls bobbing. "All the way back to the start," she said bossily. She grinned at Ellie, her green eyes shining. "This game is my best present ever because *I'm* winning!"

Laughing, Ellie slid her counter to the end of the snake, then glanced at the clock. It was Christmas afternoon and she was feeling happily full from the delicious roast turkey and Christmas pudding they'd had for lunch. She could hear Mum singing Christmas carols in the kitchen as she tidied up, and Dad was sitting at the dining table, putting together the doll's house that Santa had given Molly that morning. Ellie grinned. Christmas was her most favourite time of year, and today was going to be extra-special because soon she, Jasmine and Summer would be heading off to the Secret Kingdom to see Rosalind, the famous elf ballerina, perform her snow-globe dance!

"It's your turn," said Molly, interrupting

Ellie's thoughts.

"Sorry, I was thinking about later," Ellie said, throwing a four and moving her piece along the board.

"Me too!" Mum called from the kitchen. "I'm looking forward to going ice skating."

Ellie giggled. Mum didn't know she was thinking about the Secret Kingdom! No one knew about the magical land apart from Ellie and her best friends, Summer and Jasmine.

Ellie and her family had arranged to meet up with Summer's and Jasmine's families for the Twilight Skate at the outdoor skating rink that had been set up in Honeyvale village for the Christmas holidays. They'd get there just before three o'clock, the time when Trixi

had arranged to come and whisk Ellie, Summer and Jasmine off for another magical adventure!

"Can't wait to tell Jasmine and Summer some of your jokes, eh?" Dad said, grinning.

Ellie picked up the joke book she'd found in her stocking. "You bet," she said. "What do you get if you eat Christmas decorations?"

Dad frowned thoughtfully. "I don't know."

"Tinselitis!" giggled Ellie.

Her mum and dad laughed. "Good old Santa!" Mum said. "He always brings great presents."

"Yes," agreed Ellie. *And later on*, she thought excitedly, *I'll be able to say thank you to him!* Santa would be at Christmas Castle to watch Rosalind's snow-globe dance and Ellie could hardly wait to see him again.

"I win!" cheered Molly, jumping up and dancing round the table.

"Well done," Ellie said.

"And good timing," said Dad. "We should head over to the ice rink."

Ellie dashed out into the hall and pulled on her coat and her matching purple hat, scarf and gloves. She tucked her new joke book into her pocket, then ran up to her bedroom and grabbed the Magic Box. Hiding the box under her scarf, she raced downstairs again.

"Come on!" she cried impatiently, hopping from foot to foot as she waited for her mum and dad and Molly to get ready.

"Hold your horses," Dad said. "The ice rink's not going to suddenly disappear if we're a few minutes late."

Mum helped Molly put on her gloves, then they stepped outside into a bright, frosty afternoon with a clear blue sky and dazzling sunshine.

"Is it going to snow?" asked Molly.

"I don't think so," Mum said. "No white Christmas for us this year."

Ellie grinned as she thought of the deep snow in the Secret Kingdom. It was definitely a white Christmas there!

Jasmine and Summer were already waiting beside the ice rink when Ellie

and her family arrived. The rink had
been set up in the village square beside
Honeyvale's huge Christmas tree and the
tree-lights glinted on the ice in a rainbow
of colours.

Summer and Jasmine ran to meet Ellie.
"Happy Christmas!" they called.

"What presents did Santa bring you?" asked Ellie.

"A whole set of animal books," Summer said, beaming. "They're brilliant! And these!" She held up her hands to show them a pair of red gloves decorated with flying reindeer. "I think they look a bit like Dasher and Dancer."

"Exactly like them," said Jasmine. She pulled back her sleeve to show them the bangles that Santa had given her. They were thin silver bands that jingled when she moved her wrist. "Aren't they pretty?"

"Beautiful!" Summer and Ellie agreed.

"Santa gave me a joke book," said Ellie, pulling it out of her pocket. "What do cows say at Christmas?"

"Don't know," said Summer.

"*Mooey* Christmas!" Ellie giggled.

Jasmine and Summer laughed.

"Hurry up and get your skates on, girls," called Jasmine's mum from the ice. "You're missing all the fun."

"Coming!" they called back.

Summer's mum, stepdad and her three brothers were already gliding around the rink. Jasmine's mum and grandma were skating slowly, close to the edge, and Ellie's dad was towing Molly across the ice while Ellie's mum took photos.

"It's almost three o'clock," Summer said, grinning. "So we should get Trixi's message any minute. We'd better find somewhere to hide."

"It's lucky that no time passes while we're in the Secret Kingdom," Jasmine said. "No one will even notice that we're gone, and we can do lots of ice skating when we get back!"

They sneaked behind the Christmas tree and Ellie showed them the Magic Box hidden under her scarf. They all gazed at the mirror, eagerly waiting for it to start glowing.

The church clock began to strike three and the mirror lit up. "Right on time," giggled Ellie excitedly.

Trixi's riddle appeared in the mirror and Summer read it out:

"Girls, you know where you must go
To join us for the Christmas show!"

"We don't need the map this time," said Jasmine as they placed their palms over the green gems in the Magic Box's lid.

"We know just where the Christmas fun will be," Ellie agreed.

"The answer is Christmas Castle!" they cried together.

On With the Show!

The Magic Box flew open and a
fountain of red-and-green sparkles shot
out and spun around the Christmas
tree, making the decorations glitter and
twinkle even more brightly. A few people
on the ice rink oohed and ahhed at the
sparkling tree. They had no idea that it
was pixie magic!

Trixi appeared, flying on her holly leaf again. Today she was wearing a red party dress covered with white pom-poms and a hat made from a snowdrop. "Merry Christmas!" she cried.

"Merry Christmas to you too, Trixi!" exclaimed Jasmine. She could hardly wait to go to the Secret Kingdom and watch Rosalind's snow-globe dance.

The girls held hands, ready for their magical journey to the Secret Kingdom. They exchanged excited smiles as Trixi

tapped her beautiful pixie ring and
chanted:

"Magic, grant our Christmas wish.
The snow-globe dance we must not miss!"

Her words appeared in silvery letters
across the mirror. Then they spiralled
into the air where they broke apart and
came showering down in a twinkling
snowstorm that whirled around the girls,
lifting them off their feet.

They landed in the entrance hall of
Christmas Castle. Summer grinned as she
felt her tiara settle gently on her head –
then gasped as she realised that they were
now wearing pretty party dresses as well!
Hers was golden, Jasmine's was a rich
green with floaty skirt, and Ellie's was red

with a snowflake pattern and white fluffy trim on the sleeves and neck.

"There!" Trixi said happily. "Now you're dressed up and ready for the show!"

The girls walked into the banqueting hall with Trixi whizzing beside them on her holly leaf. Inside, everything looked

as beautiful and Christmassy as it had yesterday. Half the hall was set up like a theatre, with rows of chairs facing a great stage. The other half, where the tables had been for the Festive Feast, was now filled with cosy chairs clustered round the great fireplace where a fire crackled cheerfully. The huge Christmas

tree stretched right up to the ceiling, and the floor was scattered with brightly-coloured paper as every elf, imp and pixie child played with their presents.

One elf let off some indoor fireworks that fizzed and sparkled in the air. A brownie was bouncing a ball that changed colour every time it bounced up into the air.

The girls smiled as they looked around.

It was the most perfect Christmassy scene.
And in the middle of it all – sitting in a
large comfy chair beside the fire, with
all his reindeer lying at his feet – was
Santa!

"He looks tired," Jasmine said, as Santa
yawned and rubbed his eyes.

"No wonder," said Summer. "He's been racing round the world all night, delivering presents."

They ran across to him. "Thank you for our presents, Santa," they chorused.

"Ho, ho, ho! You're welcome!" said Santa. "You girls have been very good this year, helping the Secret Kingdom."

"I love my joke book," Ellie said, pulling it out of her pocket. "What are brown and sneak around at Christmas?" she asked.

Santa rubbed his beard thoughtfully, then shook his head.

"Mince spies," laughed Ellie.

"Ho, ho, ho!" chuckled Santa, his eyes twinkling with merriment.

Summer and Jasmine laughed too. Even Santa's reindeer joined in, giving neighing

laughs that set the bells on their harnesses jingling.

Summer bent down to stroke Dancer, a chestnut reindeer with white spots in her fur.

As Dancer nuzzled her with her warm nose, Summer felt so happy that she could burst!

King Merry came rushing over. He was wearing his Santa hat underneath his crown again and he had to hold it on with both hands to stop it falling off. "You're here!" he cried, beaming at the girls. "And just in time! Everyone take your places!" he announced. "The Christmas show's about to start."

Trixi tapped her pixie ring and all the wrapping paper disappeared. The brownies, gnomes, elves, imps, fairies and pixies rushed to their places, chattering excitedly.

"Come and sit down, then we can begin." King Merry hurried away towards the door.

"Where's he going?" Jasmine asked, puzzled.

Suddenly King Merry stopped and looked round in surprise, then turned and ran back towards them. "Wrong direction!" he chuckled as he ran past.

"It's all the Christmas excitement," giggled Trixi. "He doesn't know whether he's coming or going today!"

The lights in the hall began to dim.

"Follow me," Trixi said, flying her leaf

off towards the stage. "King Merry's saved
seats for us in the front row."

"See you all later," Ellie said to Santa
and the reindeer.

"I'll look forward to hearing more of
your jokes, Ellie," Santa called as the girls
hurried away.

As soon as they were in their seats,
the lights went out, plunging the room
into darkness. Jasmine felt a tingle of
excitement run down her back, but she
couldn't help looking round nervously.
Yesterday Queen Malice had been so
determined to ruin the show that
Jasmine couldn't help feeling worried
the wicked queen would do something
horrid again today. But there was no
sign of her.

Jasmine pushed the thought from

her mind and reached for Ellie's and Summer's hands. "Here goes!" she whispered excitedly.

"Hooray for Christmas!" cried King Merry from the darkness. "Now, on with the show!"

A Cloaked Figure

Jasmine, Summer and Ellie stared at the stage excitedly. Next to them, Trixi tapped her pixie ring and called out:

"We're all ready, so let's go –
Set the stage for the Christmas show!"

Balls of silver light appeared and floated up to the ceiling. They lit up a beautiful pool of clear blue water that had magically appeared on the stage.

It was surrounded by rocks that were covered in tiny glowing stars. Mermaids with tinsel woven into their long hair sat on the rocks, with the tips of their shimmering tails in the water.

The music began, and suddenly there was a movement from the side of the stage. Jasmine felt herself tense, then

smiled as she saw it was Rosalind, dressed in a sparkling tutu. The audience gasped as she danced onto the stage on the very tips of her toes. Everyone burst into applause as she stood in front of the mermaids and began to dance.

The mermaids sang three Christmas carols, *Away in a Rock Pool*, *Hark the Herald Mermaids Sing* and *We Wish You a Magic Christmas*, and Rosalind danced to each one, jumping and twirling in time with their beautiful voices.

"Isn't Rosalind amazing?" whispered Ellie.

"And the mermaids," Summer added dreamily. "Their voices remind me of bells tinkling."

"I could listen to them all day," Jasmine agreed happily.

When their songs were over, Rosalind danced offstage and the mermaids dived into the pool while the audience clapped and cheered. The lights went out, and when they came on again the pool had vanished. Rosalind danced back onto the stage with twenty elf children, who were dressed as snowflakes in glittering silver tops and tights.

As the music started the children started
to dance, skipping in a circle around the
twirling ballerina, then whirling across
the stage with their arms outstretched
like snowflakes fluttering in the breeze.
Finally, Rosalind gave a giant leap
and danced offstage with the little elves
following her.

When the applause died down, King
Merry leaped to his feet. "And now,"
he said, smiling happily, "the moment
you've all been waiting for… Rosalind
Daintyfeet's famous snow-globe dance!"
He waved cheerfully to Trixi, who tapped
her pixie ring.

The girls stared at the stage, waiting
for the beautiful snow-globe they'd seen
yesterday to magically appear.

"Look!" a brownie shouted, pointing up

to the ceiling.

Ellie gasped.
The snow-
globe was
slowly
floating
down onto
the stage –
with Rosalind
inside! She
had changed
in a white tutu,
covered with silver

sequins that glittered as she moved, and
gold ballet shoes tied with silver ribbons.
On her head was a sparkling diamond
tiara. As the snow-globe landed gently
on the stage, Rosalind dropped into a
beautiful curtsey.

A ripple of excitement ran through the crowd as the orchestra began to play again. Summer sat up straight in her seat in excitement.

But as the music began, a loud cackle rang out around the hall and suddenly the snow globe began to fill with the swirling tendrils of a thick black cloud. Rosalind looked panicked as the cloud surrounded her.

Then a tall figure stepped onto the stage. They were wearing a long black cloak, with the hood pulled forward to hide their face.

"I don't think this is part of the show," Jasmine said anxiously.

With another cackle, the figure threw back their hood.

"Queen Malice!" gasped Summer.

"Oh, no!" Ellie cried.

The evil queen stalked to the front of the stage, sneering nastily as everyone shrank away from her. The children in the audience slipped off their parents' laps and hid under the chairs.

"Merry Christmas!" Queen Malice cackled.

"Or should I say *Misery* Christmas?" She raised her thunderbolt staff, then banged it down hard on the stage.

A crack of thunder pealed out and echoed around the hall, setting the windows rattling. "What's she doing?" Summer said, her voice wobbling.

"Something bad I bet," replied Jasmine angrily.

Queen Malice threw back her head and began to chant a spell:

"My foolish brother's out of luck,
In the snow globe he'll be stuck –
Until you give me the one thing
That can save this silly king.
Not Christmas future or Christmas past,
The kingdom will be mine at last!"

Queen Malice finished her spell and
gazed triumphantly at the snow globe.
The smoke had gone – and King Merry
was now inside with Rosalind!

"Sister," King Merry pleaded, his voice
muffled, "let us out. It's Christmas!"

Queen Malice hooted with laughter.
"Who cares about Christmas? Not me!"

"Why don't they just open the door and come out?" asked Ellie, puzzled.

The girls watched in confusion as the little king and the beautiful ballerina started banging on the glass.

"Hang on!" Jasmine exclaimed suddenly. She narrowed her eyes, trying to see better. "The door's vanished!"

The girls exchanged horrified looks. "Queen Malice must have magicked it away," said Ellie, shocked. "Poor Rosalind and King Merry – they're trapped!"

Trapped!

"Merry Christmas, everyone!" Queen
Malice cackled again. She looked at
her brother and her dark eyes shone
with glee. Then she thumped down her
thunderbolt staff and snow started falling
heavily inside the globe.

"Oh dear," King Merry said, his
voice muffled by the glass. "Oh dearie,
dearie me."

"Once you give me what I want, I'll let them out," Queen Malice said wickedly.

"What *do* you want?" Summer asked crossly.

"Why, that's for you to work out," Queen Malice laughed. "And you'd better hurry – before my dear brother turns into a snowman!" She gave a final cackle and vanished in a puff of black smoke.

As soon as she'd gone, everyone ran over to the snow globe.

"What a disaster!" Rosalind sobbed from inside the globe.

"There, there," King Merry said gently, putting an arm around Rosalind's heaving shoulders. "Ellie, Summer and Jasmine will find a way to get us out. Won't you, my dears?" He looked at

them expectantly, his twinkly eyes full of hope.

"Of course," Jasmine said, sounding braver than she felt.

"Don't worry, Your Majesty," Ellie added. "We'll find a way to break Queen Malice's spell."

"Perhaps the door's still there, but just hidden?" Summer suggested.

The girls circled the snow globe, running their hands over the smooth glass. It felt very cold, but completely smooth. There was no sign of any opening – it was as if the door had never been there.

"The snow's getting deeper," warned Ellie. It had already reached King Merry's ankles and he and Rosalind were starting to look very cold. The little king stamped his feet and blew into his hands, trying to warm them.

"What exactly did Queen Malice say in her spell?" Ellie asked.

"Not Christmas future, or Christmas past," Jasmine remembered. "But that doesn't make sense! What can it mean?"

"Summer, you're best with words and riddles, why don't you try and work it out while we see if we can get them out another way?" Ellie suggested.

"Okay," Summer agreed. "Everyone who's good at riddles come with me!" A group of brownies, pixies, nymphs and imps followed her over to Santa's cosy spot by the fire, where they could sit and think.

"Has anyone else got any other ideas about how to get King Merry out?" Jasmine asked. "Could you use your magic, Trixi?"

Trixi looked doubtful. "I'll try," she said. "But Queen Malice's magic is much stronger than mine." She tapped her glittering pixie ring and chanted:

"Our friends are trapped, without a doubt.
Pixie magic, let them out!"

Glittering blue sparkles came bursting out of the ring. They whizzed round and round the globe and Ellie and Jasmine exchanged hopeful looks. But when the sparkles faded Rosalind and King Merry were still trapped inside. The snow was falling heavier than ever – it was almost up to their knees now!

"Never m-m-m-i-n-d," King Merry said, his teeth chattering. "I'm sure you'll thi-i-nk of somethi-i-i-ng!"

"What about Santa's magic?" asked Ellie. "That's stronger than pixie magic, isn't it?"

Santa hurried forward, his kind face creased with worry. "Ho, ho, ho, I'll do what I can," he said. "But I'm afraid I'm very tired after delivering all those presents last night." He placed both hands on the snow globe. Shutting his eyes tight,

he began to whisper:

> "Mistletoe and Ivy, Jingle Bells,
> I call on you to break this spell."

A shimmering spell of golden magic began to twinkle around his hands. It spread out slowly, warming the glass and melting any snowflake that touched it.

"I think it's working!" gasped Ellie.

But almost at once the golden magic began to lose its brightness and shrink back. Santa slumped against the snow-globe, suddenly exhausted.

"Anyone who can do magic, help with the spell!" shouted Jasmine. She and Ellie stood on either side of Santa while Trixi and all the other pixies came swooping in on their leaves. The fairies fluttered

around the snow globe too, waving
their wands.

Golden sparkles came shooting out of
wands, pixie rings and unicorn horns.

They whirled around the snow globe
and mixed with Santa's special Christmas
magic, making the golden spell surge
across the glass again.

But Queen Malice's magic was still too
strong. As Santa's golden magic vanished,
the snow-globe looked exactly the
same.

The two girls exchanged anxious looks as they helped Santa to a chair. He sank into it, worn out. "I'm so sorry," he sighed. "I wanted to help, but Queen Malice's magic is too strong even for me."

"Thanks for trying, Santa," said Ellie.

"We can't give up," Jasmine said with fierce determination. "There has to be a way of opening the snow globe. We can't let Queen Malice win!"

⌐Too Much Snow〜

Everyone looked at the snow globe in dismay. "There must be something we can do!" Ellie sighed.

"The globe's made of glass!" one elf cried suddenly. "Maybe we can smash it open."

"I can help with that," said a gentle voice behind them.

Turning, Ellie saw their friend Silvertail, a beautiful unicorn with a golden horn and a pale pink coat. "Perhaps our horns will be strong enough to break the glass," she said, tossing her long silver mane.

"King Merry, Rosalind, go behind the gingerbread house," Jasmine shouted. "You'll be safe there."

King Merry held Rosalind's hand as they waded through the snow. They squeezed in behind the gingerbread house

until they were completely hidden from sight.

The girls stepped back, crossing their fingers for luck as Silvertail and the other unicorns charged at the snow globe. Their golden horns clattered against it, but instead of breaking through, they sent the globe spinning down the hall! King Merry and Rosalind somersaulted over and over, and people dived out of the way as the globe rolled past, knocking over chairs and spinning past the great Christmas tree. "Whoooooaaa!" King Merry yelled as they spun.

"Stop it! Quick!" gasped Ellie. Two elves caught it as it rolled past and pushed it back the right way up.

Ellie and Jasmine rushed over to the globe.

"Are you all right?" Jasmine called. All they could see was the ballerina's tutu and King Merry's crown sticking out of the snow.

King Merry got shakily to his feet, then fell over onto his bottom. Rosalind scrambled up daintily and helped the little king out of the snowdrift. "Good thing I'm used to twirling around," she joked bravely.

"We've got it!" came a shout from across the hall. Summer ran over, flapping a piece of paper in her hand. "A time that's not the future or the past – the *present*! Queen Malice wants all our Christmas presents!"

There was a horrified gasp. Then everyone starting talking at once.

One of the little elf boys who had been in the snowflake dance began to cry. "Santa gave me a red train," he sobbed. "I don't want to give it to nasty Queen Malice."

"But you want to help King Merry, don't you, darling," said his mother, kneeling down to hug him. He gave a weepy nod.

"Of course we'll give up our presents," everyone agreed.

"Do-o-o-on't worry about us!" called Rosalind, her teeth chattering. "We-e-e'll be all o-o-o-kay."

But everyone could see that they weren't all right at all. The snow was almost touching King Merry's chin now, and Rosalind's nose was turning blue.

"Can you climb onto the roof of the gingerbread house, out of the snow?" Ellie called to them.

King Merry made his way to the Christmas tree, sending the snow flying up in flurries as he pushed through it. Then he helped Rosalind up onto the roof of the gingerbread house before clambering up himself.

"They're out of harm's way for now," Jasmine said anxiously. "But it won't be long before the snow reaches the roof!"

"We've got to get them out before that happens," Summer said.

"Let's start collecting up the presents," Trixi sighed. "Santa, can we use your sack?"

Santa nodded sadly. "Of course," he agreed. "But my sack is meant for giving people presents, not taking them away." He pointed at the floor and an enormous red sack appeared.

"I'll go first," said Ellie. She placed her joke book in the sack.

Jasmine slipped off her bangles, and Summer took her new gloves out of her pocket. They placed them in the sack too. "I love those gloves," sighed Summer. Then she glanced at King Merry and Rosalind who were huddled on the roof of the gingerbread house. "But I'd rather have King Merry and Rosalind safe than any present!"

One by one, all the brownies, unicorns and nymphs trudged up to the sack, their

shoulders slumped as they handed over
the colourful scarves, toys and books that
Santa had given them.

The imps and the elves came next. The
little elf bravely gave Summer his shiny
red train, then hurried away in tears.

Trixi was the last to put her Christmas
present into the sack. It was a tiny
rainbow brooch that twinkled as it
caught the light. "There," she said.
"That's everything."

"Um…help!" King Merry cried.

The girls had been so busy packing the presents that they hadn't looked at the snow-globe for a while, but now they saw that the snow had risen much higher. The Christmas tree and the gingerbread house were completely buried and poor King Merry and Rosalind were standing on the roof, up to their ears in snow. King Merry was holding a piece of candy cane from the window frame and swishing it to and fro through the snow to keep it from piling up around their heads.

"Hold on!" Jasmine called, gathering up the top of the sack. "That's all the presents, Queen Malice!" she called in a loud voice. "We give these to you!"

Summer stared at the snowglobe, holding her breath — but nothing happened. As the snow reached the top of the snowglobe, King Merry and Rosalind disappeared completely!

Presents for Queen Malice

"It didn't work!" Trixi sobbed.

"Wait!" Jasmine felt a surge of hope.
"What's that noise?" There was a deep
crash, the sound of a thunderbolt, and the
snow-globe cracked in two!

"Queen Malice's spell has broken!" Ellie
sighed in relief.

Snow poured out of the globe, and
Rosalind and King Merry came with it,
coughing and spluttering. Summer, Ellie
and Jasmine ran to help them up.

"Are you okay?" asked Summer, brushing snow from King Merry's hat.

"N-n-not too b-bad," King Merry stuttered through chattering teeth.

"Tha-an-nks to yo-o-ou," Rosalind added with a shaky smile.

The girls helped them both into seats close to the fire and an elf butler came hurrying over with two mugs of steaming cocoa on a silver tray. Another butler brought thick blankets and the girls

wrapped them around the little king and the beautiful ballerina.

Just then, the fairy lights on the enormous Christmas tree dimmed. There was a deafening crack of thunder and a lightning flash so bright that it hurt the girls' eyes to look at it. Suddenly Queen Malice was standing back on the stage, while her Storm Sprites flew above her in a ragged circle, grinning nastily.

"So," shrieked the horrid queen, "you worked it out after all. I was hoping my brother and that pesky ballerina would be ice cubes by now. But at least I have your presents!" She looked down at the bulging sack and her face lit up in an evil smile. Stepping down off the stage, she picked up an armful of presents and flung them up in the air.

"My train!" sobbed the little elf boy as his shiny red train smashed on the floor.

"Wrong!" snapped Queen Malice. "It's *my* train!"

One of the Storm Sprites seized a pair of purple earmuffs. Another Storm Sprite tried to snatch them from him.

"I want them, bat-ears!" he shouted.

"I saw them first, big nose!" roared the first, trying to push him away.

They fluttered
above the sack
as they fought
in midair,
yanking the
earmuffs
to and fro
between
them.

"This is the worst
Christmas ever," an elf sighed.

King Merry held the mug in his frozen
hands to warm them. "Christmas is
ruined," he said sadly. "You should have
left us inside the snow globe."

"Nobody could have enjoyed
Christmas without you," said Ellie.
"Besides, Christmas isn't all about
presents."

"It's about friends," Summer said.

"And fun and games!" Jasmine added.

"And dancing!" Rosalind smiled.

"Enough!" Queen Malice clapped her hands. "No more of this goody-goody goodwill! Storm Sprites, pick up the sack. Let's take all my new things back to Thunder Castle so we can *break* them!"

This is so unfair, Ellie thought as the sprites flew into the air, struggling to pull the full sack after them. "It's not fair that someone so mean should get so many presents," she sighed.

"Hang on!" Jasmine gasped. "That gives me an idea!"

Ellie and Summer looked at Jasmine hopefully as she called, "Santa, has Queen Malice been naughty or nice this year?"

Santa chuckled loudly. "Ho, ho, ho! Naughty, of course!" Suddenly the presents in the sack began to glow with golden light.

The Storm Sprites stopped in midair, eyeing them warily.

"What's happening?" screeched Queen Malice.

"Everyone knows naughty people don't deserve presents," Santa reminded her. The golden glow grew brighter and silver sparkles began to flicker all around the bulging sack.

The Storm Sprites dropped the sack in fear and it fell to the floor. As it hit the ground it burst open – but instead of presents, out poured knobbly lumps of glistening black coal!

Present Magic

"COAL?" screeched Queen Malice "Where are my presents? Turn them back!"

"Ho, ho, ho, I'm afraid I can't," chuckled Santa, his eyes twinkling with mischief. "Present magic is in every gift I deliver, so if I accidentally give a gift to somebody naughty, the magic turns it into coal."

Queen Malice stamped her foot in fury. "You can all keep your stupid coal!" she yelled. "At least *you* don't have any presents either! One day I will rule this kingdom, just you wait and see. And the first thing I'll do is cancel Christmas!"

Beckoning to her Storm Sprites, she banged down her thunderbolt staff and vanished.

The Storm Sprites flapped towards an open window. "Wait!" called Santa, holding up some red-and-green striped Christmas stockings. "I know Queen Malice won't let you hang stockings up in Thunder Castle, but these are for you."

The Storm Sprites swooped down, barging each other aside in their hurry to reach Santa first.

"There's no need to push. There's one each," he said, handing them out.

"A giant mince pie!" cheered the first Storm Sprite, pulling it out of his stocking. "My favourite!"

"No, mince pies are *my* favourite!"

another Storm Sprite shouted.

Arguing furiously, they flapped their bat-like wings and flew out of the

window and away.

"Thank goodness they've gone," Summer said, relieved. "But what a shame all the presents have turned into coal."

Everyone stared at the sack of coal miserably.

Suddenly the pile of coal began to glow and silver sparkles flickered around it once more. "What's happening?" gasped Jasmine.

"Wait and see," Santa replied with a grin.

Slowly the lumps of coal began to change. Their blackness melted into bright colours and the knobbly lumps twisted into new shapes. "The coal's turning back into presents!" cheered Ellie. The red train was right on the top of

the nearest sack and she lifted it out and handed it to the little elf boy.

"Thank you!" he cried happily, hugging it tight.

"Why did the presents change back, Santa?" Summer asked, as the girls helped

him give them out.

"Because everyone here has been good this year," explained Santa. "The present magic worked in reverse because the presents are back with their rightful owners."

The girls grinned at each other.

"There are just four presents left," Santa said at last. "Trixi, this is yours." He handed over her tiny brooch.

"Thank you, Santa," she said, smiling, as she pinned it to her dress.

Santa gave Summer, Ellie and Jasmine their presents too. "Thanks, Santa," they said, hugging him.

"Let's finish the show!" Rosalind said.

"Oh, yes," King Merry said, with a beaming smile. "But what about your snow-globe, my dear?"

"I don't think I want to go back in the snow-globe any time soon!" Rosalind laughed.

Trixi tapped her pixie ring. The broken snow-globe began to glow with golden light, then disappeared.

Rosalind ran daintily onto the stage and the orchestra struck up. Everyone rushed back to their chairs.

"Queen Malice didn't spoil anything," Ellie said happily as the girls settled back

into their front-row seats. "It's like she was never here!"

The girls watched spellbound as Rosalind spun round on one leg, then she gracefully leaped and skipped across the stage.

As the ballerina twisted and twirled, Summer grabbed both her friends by the hand. She was so happy that they'd managed to stop Queen Malice from ruining the Christmas show. She glanced round at the unicorns, elves, pixies and magical creatures in the audience, all watching Rosalind happily, and felt a surge of joy. Then she looked back at the stage, where the beautiful ballerina was spinning. Rosalind got faster and faster, her gorgeous tutu glittering in the light, then she lifted up into the air. Her famous air pirouette!

When the pirouette ended there was a moment of perfect silence. "Amazing!" breathed Jasmine, smiling delightedly.

Then the audience rose to their feet, clapping and cheering. "Bravo!" they cried. "Well done, Rosalind!"

Rosalind curtseyed and smiled at the audience. "The Christmas show wouldn't have gone ahead if it hadn't been for three girls from the Other Realm," said Rosalind, smiling.

"And nobody would have had any presents either," called a gnome.

"Ellie, Jasmine and Summer, will you please come up onstage?" Rosalind asked.

The girls exchanged surprised glances, then giggled as they ran up onstage. Rosalind nodded at the orchestra, and they started to play.

"But I can't dance!" Summer panicked. Suddenly she and Ellie were surrounded

by the elf snowflakes. As Rosalind showed
Jasmine a proper ballerina twirl, Summer
and Ellie jigged about with the elf
children until they were breathless with
laughter.

"Hooray for Summer, Jasmine and
Ellie!" King Merry cried as he came on

stage with Santa, followed by Trixi on her holly leaf. "They've saved Christmas again!"

Rosalind gave them each a hug as the audience clapped wildly. "Hooray!" they cheered. "Hooray!" Summer felt her face go hot with embarrassment, but Jasmine started curtsying just like Rosalind!

"Now, on with the Christmas fun!" King Merry announced when the applause had died down. "Everyone for hot chocolate and carols by the fire!"

"It's turned out to be a brilliant Christmas Day after all," Ellie said happily as they stepped off stage.

"And Christmas isn't over yet," said Jasmine, grinning at Ellie and Summer. "We've still got a whole afternoon of fun waiting for us back home."

"I think I'm ready to go home now," Summer said, suddenly wanting to be with her family again. "It's been amazing here, but Christmas is brilliant at home, too."

"Of course," King Merry agreed, his eyes twinkling.

"I'll see you next year." Santa grinned. "I have a feeling that you three will definitely be on my 'nice' list!"

"Thank you so much, girls," Trixi said, flying her leaf over to kiss them on the tips of their noses.

"Merry Christmas,

everyone!" Summer, Ellie and Jasmine
cried together as they waved goodbye.
Then they held hands and Trixi tapped

her pixie ring. A cloud of red-and-green
sparkles came whizzing out and whirled
round the girls.

"Happy Christmas," all the elves,
brownies and unicorns called as the

girls were lifted off their feet and swept
back home. As the sparkles vanished
they found themselves back behind the
Christmas tree next to the ice rink.

Their families were whizzing round the
ice, laughing and giggling, completely
unaware that the girls had just come
back from their own Christmas
adventure. Ellie, Summer and Jasmine

smiled at one another, pulled on their skates, and stepped out on to the ice together.

"Watch this," said Jasmine, spinning on one foot. "I'm copying one of Rosalind's brilliant spins." She wobbled and slipped

over, falling on her bottom with a bump.
"Whoops, I think I need a bit more
practice," she giggled.

Ellie and Summer helped her up. "What
an amazing Christmas Day we've had!"
Ellie said, grinning.

"It's been great," agreed Jasmine.

"Christmas is brilliant," Summer said,
linking arms with her two best friends.
"And a Secret Kingdom Christmas is
even better!"

Join Ellie, Summer and Jasmine on their next Secret Kingdom adventure...

Puppy Fun

Read on for a sneak peek!

An Amazing Adventure

"It's almost half term!" Jasmine twirled round in the spring sunshine as she walked back from school with her best friends, Summer and Ellie. "Just a few more days. I can't wait!"

"It will be great to spend it together," said Ellie, her red curls bouncing on her shoulders as she skipped after Jasmine. "We can go swimming and play in the park and have sleepovers!"

Jasmine's hazel eyes sparkled. "Do you think we'll also get to visit somewhere else?"

"I hope so!" said Ellie with a smile, knowing exactly what she meant. The three girls shared an amazing secret. They had a Magic Box that transported them to an enchanted land called the Secret Kingdom! The Magic Box had been made by King Merry, the ruler of the magical land. He needed the girls' help to protect the kingdom from his mean sister, Queen Malice, who wanted to rule and make everyone as miserable as she was! The girls had helped the king many times now, and enjoyed lots of incredible adventures with the most amazing magical creatures.

Suddenly it dawned on Ellie that Summer wasn't joining in the conversation. She looked round and saw their friend was tugging anxiously at the end of one of her blonde pigtails as she hurried along the pavement. Ellie frowned. "Are you okay, Summer?"

"I'm a bit worried about Rosa," Summer admitted. Her mum had taken their cat, Rosa, to the vet's that day because she hadn't been eating her food. "I know Mum said she would be fine but I can't help worrying."

"We should head to your house straight away and find out what the news is," said Jasmine understandingly.

"Definitely," agreed Ellie.

"Thanks," Summer said gratefully, and the three friends ran all the way back to her house.

"How's Rosa?" The words tumbled out of Summer as soon as her mum opened the door.

"She's absolutely fine," Mrs Hammond said, smiling. "The vet checked her over and said there is absolutely nothing to worry about at all." Her smile broadened. "In fact, she's never been better!"

"That's brilliant!" Summer was so relieved Rosa was okay. "Where is she now?"

"She's upstairs on your bed." Summer's mum smiled.

The three girls ran upstairs. Rosa was curled up on Summer's duvet cover. She lifted her little black head as they came running in. Summer stroked her and Rosa purred loudly.

"I'm so glad you're all right," Summer said, kissing the top of Rosa's head.

"She looks happy to see you," said Jasmine, sitting down and stroking the cat's soft paws.

Listening to Rosa purring, Ellie grinned. "Hey, Summer. I know what Rosa's favourite colour is – and it's the same as mine."

"What? Green?" asked Summer, puzzled.

Ellie grinned. "No, *purr*-ple of course!"

Summer and Jasmine giggled. Ellie crouched down and tickled Rosa under the chin. "I'm glad you're all right, Rosa."

As she petted the little cat, Ellie's knees bumped against something hard under the bed. "Is this the Magic Box?" Ellie asked, pulling out a pink bag.

"Yes," said Summer. "I keep it in there so my brothers won't see it if they come into my room."

Ellie carefully took the Magic Box out of the pink bag. She stroked the wooden sides. They were carved with all sorts of magical creatures and studded with green gems. The lid of the box had a mirror on it and inside was a magic map of the Secret Kingdom that King Merry had given them and lots of other magical gifts, including a silver unicorn horn that let them talk to animals and an icy hourglass that could stop time!

"Oh, I do hope we get to go to the

Secret Kingdom again soon," Ellie said longingly.

As she spoke, a flash of light ran across the mirrored lid. Rosa sat up on the bed with a surprised miaow. The box began to glow and a string of words swirled over the shining lid.

"There's a new message for us!" gasped Ellie.

Jasmine and Summer jumped off the bed and joined her on the white rug. Even Rosa jumped off the bed! The little cat sniffed at the sparkling box curiously while Ellie read out the words:

"Hello, dear friends, how do you do?
We are really missing you!
Look for turrets where rubies glow,
And come and see a magical show!"

As Ellie read out the last word, there was a bright flash of light and the box's lid opened. The magical map of the Secret Kingdom floated out and unfolded itself in front of their eyes. It wasn't like a normal map — all the pictures on it moved! There were mermaids swimming in the sea and unicorns cantering through lush meadows, brownies skiing down a mountain covered in pink snow and golden flags flying from the pink turrets of the Enchanted Palace.

Usually the girls had to work out where in the kingdom the riddle wanted them to go, but today there was only one place it could be talking about! The pink walls and turrets of King Merry's Enchanted Palace were studded with glittering red rubies. The girls eagerly put their hands on the green gems of the box.

"Are you ready?" said Jasmine.

The others nodded. "King Merry's Enchanted Palace!" they all cried.

Read

Puppy Fun

to find out what
happens next!

Secret Kingdom

Be in on the secret.
Collect them all!

Series 1

When Jasmine, Summer and Ellie discover the magical land of the Secret Kingdom, a whole world of adventure awaits!

Series 2

Wicked Queen Malice has cast a spell to turn King Merry into a toad! Can the girls find six magic ingredients to save him?

Secret Kingdom

Swan Palace

ROSIE BANKS

Wildflower Wood

ROSIE BANKS

Snow Bear Sanctuary

ROSIE BANKS

Phoenix Festival

ROSIE BANKS

Fancy Dress Party

ROSIE BANKS

Jewel Cavern

ROSIE BANKS

Series 3

When Queen Malice releases six fairytale baddies into the Secret Kingdom, it's up to the girls to find them!

Have you read all the books in Series Four?

Puppy Fun

Magic Seal

Glitter Bird

Rainbow Lion

Meet the magical Animal Keepers of the Secret Kingdom, who spread fun, friendship, kindness and bravery throughout the land

Secret Kingdom

Collect all the sparkling Secret Kingdom special
stories - two magical adventures in one!

☐ Got it   ☐ Got it   ☐ Got it

☐ Got it   ☐ Got it   ☐ Got it

☐ Got it   ☐ Got it

Secret Kingdom

A magical world of
friendship and fun!

Join the Secret Kingdom Club at

www.secretkingdombooks.com

and enjoy games, sneak peeks and lots more!

You'll find great activities, competitions, stories
and games, plus a special newsletter for
Secret Kingdom friends!